por Linnea.

Ryan L.
12/13/00

SHAQ
AND THE
BEAN-STALK
AND OTHER
VERY TALL TALES

BY SHAQUILLE O'NEAL
Illustrated by Shane W. Evans

Cartwheel
·B·O·O·K·S·®

SCHOLASTIC INC.

New York   Toronto   London   Auckland   Sydney   Mexico City   New Delhi   Hong Kong

I dedicate this book to Chexy, Chutie, Zakaya, Hilkiah, Tyler, Guru and A'Shana, Matthew, Aliyah and Michael, Marcus and Quintin, Anthony and Elio, Thomas and Sam, just a few of the beautiful children. And to all the rest of you, I dedicate peace and love and respect.

I personally and actively support Reading Is Fundamental (RIF), Boys & Girls Clubs of America, Athletes & Entertainers For Kids (AEFK), City of Hope, and the California Mentoring Initiative (CMI). I encourage all parents to read to their children whenever and wherever.

Jimmy Preller and Shane Evans helped me with this book. Thanks, guys.

— Shaquille O'Neal

I would like to thank GOD, and dedicate this book to my mom and dad, family and friends. THANK YOU ALL for your support.
PEACE and LOVE.

— Shane W. Evans

Text copyright © 1999 by Shaquille O'Neal
Illustrations by Shane W. Evans
Photographs of Shaquille O'Neal by Jerry Avenaim

Library of Congress Cataloging-in-Publication Data

O'Neal, Shaquille.
Shaq and the beanstalk and other very tall tales / by Shaquille O'Neal.
p. cm.
"Cartwheel books."
Summary: Basketball star Shaquille O'Neal relates updated versions of five fairy tales linked together, in each of which he plays a major role: Shaq and the Beanstalk; Little Red Riding Shaq; Shaq and the Three Bears; Shaq's New Clothes; and Shaq and the Three Billy Goats Gruff.

ISBN 0-590-91823-0
[1. Fairy tales. 2. O'Neal, Shaquille—fiction.] I. Evans. Shane, ill. II. Title.
PZ8.05885Sh 1999
[Fic]—dc21   98-52007
CIP   AC

10 9 8 7 6 5 4 3 2 1   9/9 0/0 01 02 03

Printed in Singapore   46
First printing, September 1999

Book design by Elizabeth B. Parisi

Contents

Dear Reader,

As you can probably guess, I used to be a kid myself. I wasn't always seven feet tall. I didn't always weigh three hundred pounds. And I certainly didn't start out as a pro basketball player.

I was lucky. I grew up in a loving home where my parents read to me a lot. Even today, those are some of my favorite memories. Sitting snugly on my mother's lap, listening to her read a wonderful story. Even though I loved the pictures, I would sometimes close my eyes and let the words pour over me like the words to a song.

With each story, I would visit new worlds and meet new characters. And I suppose that my favorite stories were the classic folktales, like "Jack and the Beanstalk," "Little Red Riding Hood," and "The Emperor's New Clothes."

I believe everyone has their own stories to tell. These are mine. I hope they make you smile!

Your friend,

Shaq 34

Shaquille O'Neal

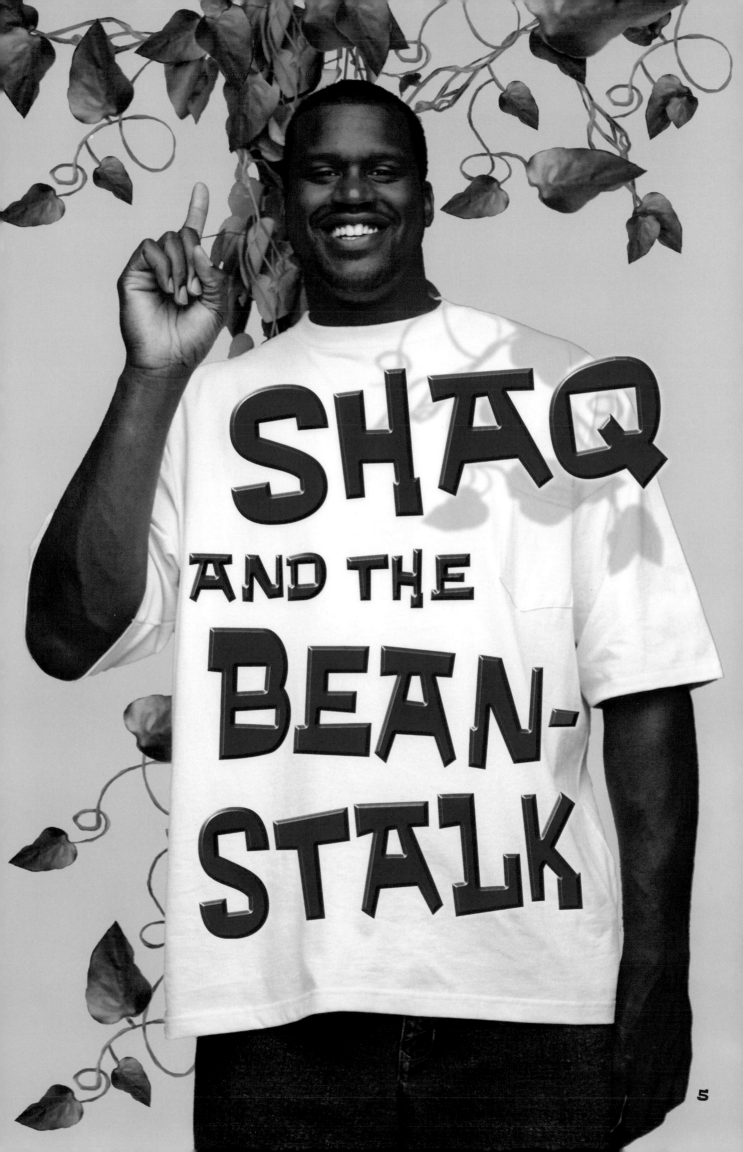

IT **SEEMS** like everybody has heard the story of "Jack and the Beanstalk." It used to be one of my favorites. But that was before I met a real giant. **Believe it!**

He was one huge, scary-looking guy. Anyway, now I have my own beanstalk story.

I call it "Shaq and the Beanstalk" and it goes like this….

When I was a little guy, just seven or eight years old, I was a Big-Time Fussy Eater.

Sure, I liked candy and pizza and pancakes and hot dogs well enough. But when it came to vegetables, I'd just as soon eat one of my smelly old basketball socks. I wouldn't eat broccoli. I sneered at cauliflower. I held my nose when spinach appeared on my plate. But one day everything changed. Right then and there, I guess you could say I became a World Champion Vegetable Eater.

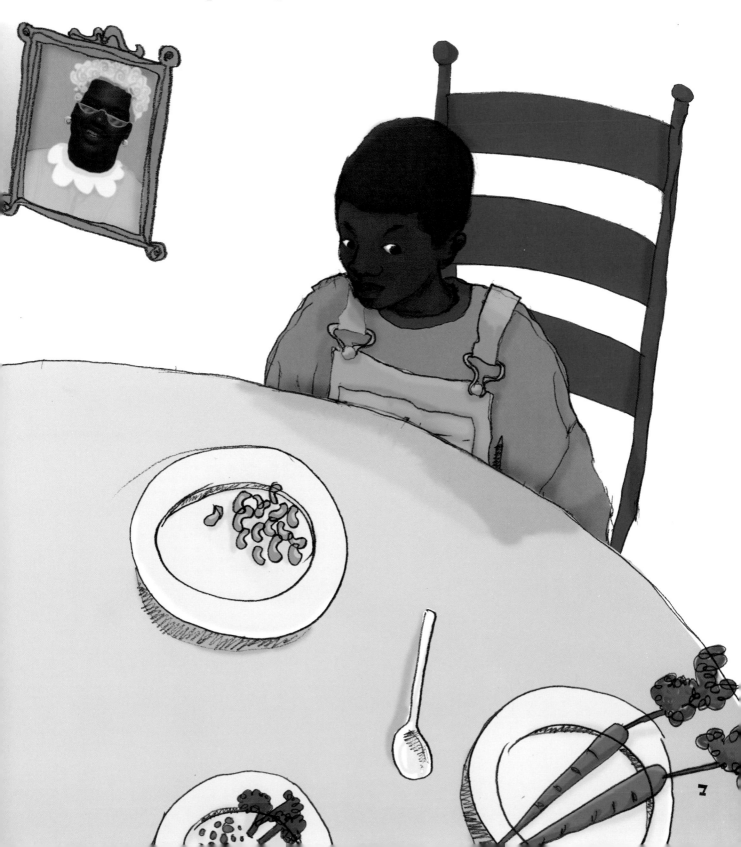

Here's what happened....

One night at dinner, I was playing with my lima beans, wishing they would disappear.

Problem was, we had a rule in my house: *No dessert unless you finish your dinner*. That meant—all your dinner, even if it included yucky green lima beans.

To make things worse, we were going to have one of my all-time favorite desserts—my great-grandmother's homemade pound cake.

What did I do? You guessed it.

When my parents weren't looking, I tossed those lima beans right out the window! They landed in the garden.

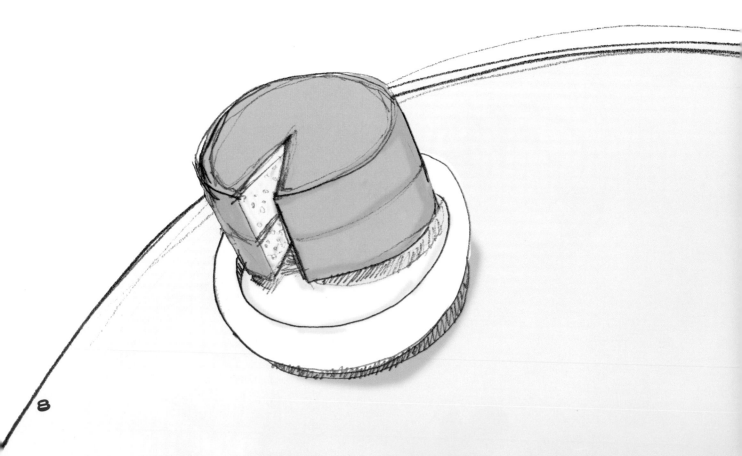

I sat down to a plate of the best pound cake in the world, all the while thinking that I was pretty smart.

But let me tell you, those lima beans nearly got me flattened like a pancake. **Believe it!**

When I woke up the next morning, I looked out the window and saw a great big plant growing high into the clouds. It was in the exact spot where I'd tossed the lima beans! Now the day before, I'd banged my head in a pick-up basketball game. So at first I thought that my mind was playing tricks on me. After all, who ever heard of a gigantic lima bean plant?

I got out of bed, ate breakfast, and forgot all about that crazy stalk outside the window. But when I ran outside to play, there it was again.

The thing is, it was a Saturday, so there wasn't any school. I looked at that lima bean stalk and figured, *Okay, what the heck.*

In no time at all, I was climbing higher and higher. Past the tallest buildings, past a gaggle of geese flying in a perfect **V**. I was so high that I started getting dizzy. But I kept right on climbing because I like to finish things once I start them. Just like with basketball, I play hard till the final buzzer.

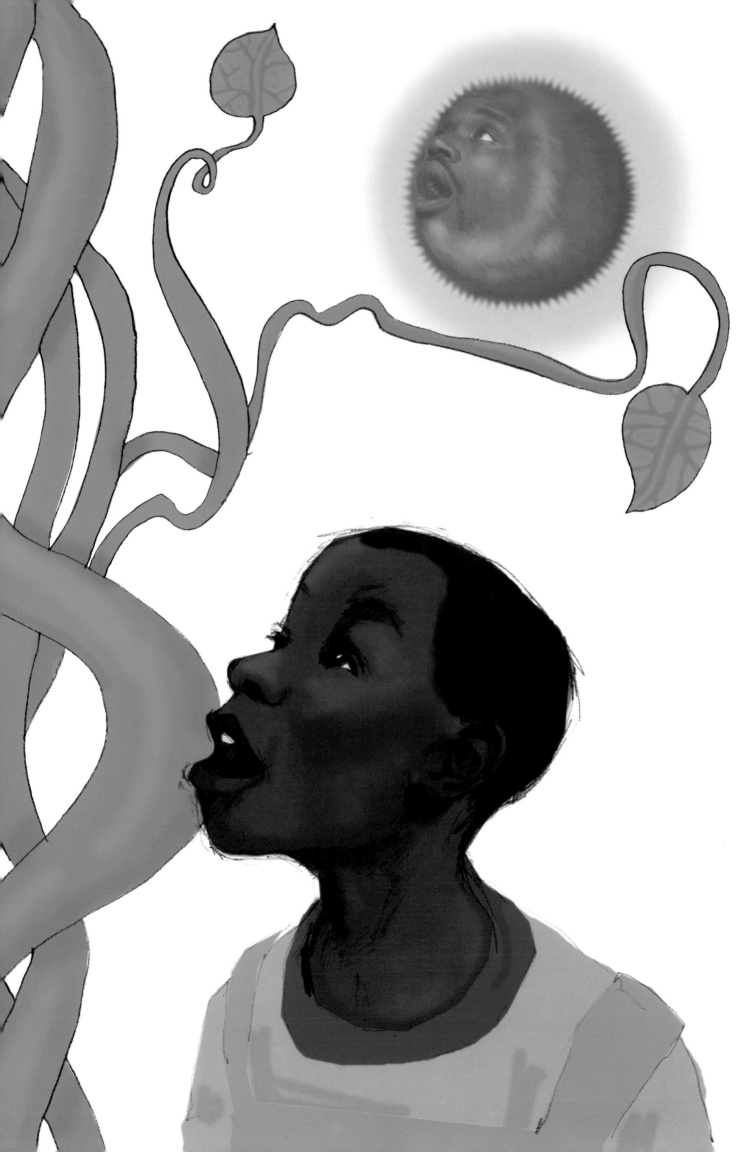

Finally I got to the top. It was pretty strange, I'll tell
you what. I was in another world, where everything looked
like the pictures in a storybook. No trash, no ugly billboards,
and no noisy cars. In the distance, I saw a glistening castle
built on the clouds. Now that's something you just don't
see every day. I figured I'd check it out. And, to tell you the
honest truth, all that climbing made me hungry. I was
hoping to catch a snack.

I walked and walked until I came to a humongous wooden door. I couldn't even reach the doorknob. So *bangity-bangity-bang,* I knocked. In a minute a deep voice, as loud as thunder, boomed:

Fee-Fie-Foe-Fum!
I smell the socks of a little man.
Be he clean, or be he smelly,
I'll soon have him in my belly.

The door swung open, and there before me stood the biggest Big Man I'd ever seen. I'll tell you, if this guy had skills, he would have done well in the NBA. Anyway, the giant stomped his foot and yelled, "Not another one of you pesky Little People! I'll eat you up!"

Now I've done some dumb things in my life. But I wasn't about to wait to see what happened next. So quick as a flash, I tied the laces of his shoes together. Then I raced between his legs into the castle.

Well, that giant tried to take a step and—
whoosh—he tripped and fell with a thunderous thud.
After a minute his face turned red, then purple, then blue.
He was plenty mad. The giant fumbled to untie his laces.
I'm not sure what he did next—because I was too busy
zooming off into the next room.

Let me tell you, he had me running all over that castle. Up the stairs, down the stairs. Into the kitchen, out of the kitchen. Man, I felt like I was running a fast break with the Lakers!

When I ran into one room, I saw the weirdest thing. It was a hen, sitting in a nest. Underneath her was a pile of golden…basketballs.

That's right — you heard me. *Golden basketballs!*

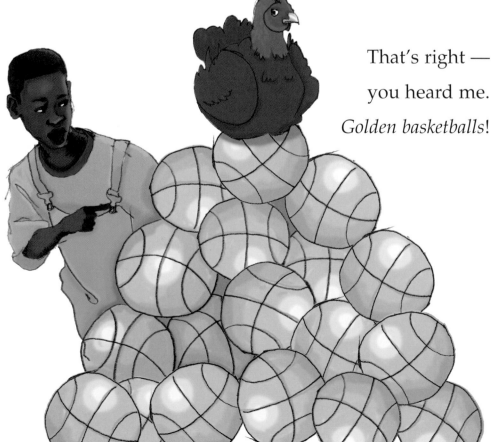

Yep, this was no ordinary hen. I snatched up a basketball and took aim. Let me stop and say one thing right now: I have always believed that fighting is the loser's way out. You get nowhere using violence. It's always better to talk your problems out. But this giant didn't seem to be in the mood for conversation. I had to fight back.

So—*WHAP!*—I hurled the golden basketball right between the big fella's eyes. Lights out! The giant went down for the count.

After that, the hen got sort of nervous. She started flapping her wings like crazy. Then she raced out the front door.

Oh well, I had other things to worry about.

Maybe another guy might have crept away with some of the giant's gold. But that's not my style—I don't take things that don't belong to me. Even if they are solid-gold basketballs!

Instead, I found some rope and tied up that giant until he couldn't move.

The giant's eyes slowly opened. He looked at me and boomed in a loud voice:

Fee-Fie-Foe-Fum!
I say if you're peanut butter,
or if you're jelly,
I'll soon have you
in my belly.

Of course I laughed. Because, hey, this particular giant was all tied up with no place to go. "Don't be ridiculous," I said. "I'd give you a stomachache."

The giant tried his best to escape. But I tie my knots good and tight, just like my dad, Sarge, taught me to. Finally the giant gave up.

Soon we got to talking. It seems this giant—his name was George—never had any visitors. That's because he hated Little People. Little People like me. Here's the thing: This giant's uncle Max once ran into some trouble with a little fellow. You probably know this rascal's name. That's right— it was Jack himself.

If you remember the story, Jack climbed up the beanstalk and did some horrible things to that giant. Think about it: Jack stole the giant's gold coins. He stole the hen that lays golden eggs. He took the giant's prized magic harp. And then Jack chopped down the beanstalk—right when the giant was climbing down it!

Ever since, all the giants far and wide have kept their doors locked. No visitors allowed.

I told George that all Little People weren't like Jack. "Look at me," I said. "I'm a nice guy. And to prove it, I'll even untie you."

So I did. But when George stood up, he was dizzy. He rubbed his head, right where I'd nailed him with the golden basketball.

Just then George saw the empty nest. "Here, chick, chick, chick," He called out. "Here, my little chickie!"

"Are you looking for that hen?" I asked.

George nodded.

"Well, she ran out the front door—fast as lightning."

George's face turned three shades of red. "That was my prize hen!" he screamed. "You made her run away!"

I gulped. I was thinking that maybe I shouldn't have untied George after all.

He said, "Now George is mad. George likes to STOMP when he's mad. My uncle Max was right," he added. "You Little People are nothing but trouble."

Things weren't looking too good for me. George was one angry giant. So I said, "Listen, big fella, I'll prove to you that not all Little People are trouble. I'll find your hen."

It was a deal. If I found the Hen That Lays Golden Basketballs, George wouldn't stomp me. Then he added one more thing. He said, "I was supposed to deliver cookies to my dear, sweet old granny. But now I can't. So you'll have to."

Sure, I wasn't crazy about becoming the giant's delivery boy. But it sure beat getting stomped like a grape. Plus, it sounded easy enough. All I had to do was deliver a basket of cookies to his grandmother. Then I'd go and find that hen. How hard could that be?

As I left for my journey, I turned and called to the big fella, "I'll be back with that hen, George, I promise—right after I deliver that gift basket to your dear, sweet old granny."

As it turned out, my simple errand turned out to be quite an adventure. Read on and you'll see what I mean.

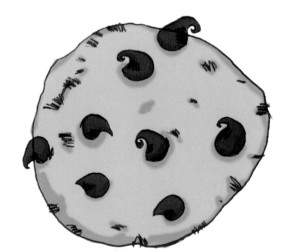

AFTER LEAVING

George, I set off — *hum-dee-dum-dum* — into the green forest.

Soon it began to get chilly. I was glad to have borrowed a red cape from George. I pulled the hood down over my head.

Birds sang and the wind whistled through the trees. Friendly animals scampered all around me. But as I trudged deeper into the forest, I noticed an eerie silence. The birds no longer sang. The happy squirrels had disappeared. Even the wind stopped whistling. I wrapped the cape even tighter around my shoulders and trudged on. After all, a promise is a promise.

Suddenly, an oily voice broke the silence. "Yo, Little Red Riding Hood. What are you doing back in the forest?"

A large wolf stepped out from behind a tree. Of course, I knew who he was. I'd read about him in books. I was staring into the face of the Big Bad Wolf. Then I remembered my cape and the hood that covered my head. Clearly, the wolf had mistaken me for someone else. I decided to play along.

I made my voice high like a little girl's. "Oh, hello, Wolf," I said. "I am off to my granny's house to deliver some cookies."

"How sweet you are, Little Red Riding Hood," the wolf purred. "Is your granny still living in the old place, near the stream?"

"Yes, Mr. Wolf," I said. Then I added, "You aren't up to your old tricks again, are you?"

"Oh no," the wolf protested. "I've turned over a

new leaf. Now people call me the Big *Good* Wolf."

His eyes twinkled devilishly. "I'm quite pleased to report that those days of crime and nastiness are far behind me."

I noticed something else behind him. The wolf's claws were crossed behind his back!

"I used to be a Big Bad Wolf," the wolf continued.

"But now I'm just a big softy. Say," he suddenly exclaimed. "I really should apologize for that unfortunate business with your granny and the woodcutter a while back. It was absolutely inexcusable of me.

"But I'm a changed wolf now," he continued. "Lately, I like nothing better than to think pretty thoughts and sniff dandelions all day. That is, when I'm not busy helping old ladies across the street."

Likely story, I thought to myself. After all, as everyone knows, there are no streets in the deep dark woods. The wolf must have figured that Little Red Riding Hood was a real sucker. Little did he realize that Shaq is nobody's lollipop.

"I'll deliver your cookies for you," the wolf said. He snatched the basket from my hands and turned away.

"Oh, thank you, Big Good Wolf," I called in a high voice. "Please give my granny a kiss when you get there."

He was soon out of sight, headed to George's granny's house. I was sure he had something unpleasant in mind. But as my daddy always told me, you can't sit around and let bad things happen. You've got to do something to make things right. Quickly, I raced along the shortcut to Granny's house.

Huffing and puffing from my run, I came to a small cottage nestled beneath the pines. A babbling stream flowed beside it.

I knocked on the door.

A frail voice answered, "George, is that you?"

I called back, "No, ma'am. My name is Shaquille. Your grandson, George, sent me."

The door swung open, and there stood a kindly old woman. "Any friend of my grandson's is welcome here," she said.

I blinked. "I thought you'd be taller," I said.

She laughed softly. "We're not all giants in our family. We're like shirts. Some of us are regular size, others are extra-large. George is an extra-large." Then she added, "And by the looks of you, it seems like you might grow up to be an extra-large yourself."

I quickly told her about the Big Bad Wolf. We made a plan. After all, sometimes it takes a trick of your own to beat a trickster. I hid Granny in the closet. But not before I borrowed her nightcap, bathrobe, slippers, and reading glasses. I jumped into the bed and pulled the comforter up to my neck.

In seconds there was a sharp rap on the door.

"Who is it?" I answered in my shakiest old lady voice.

An oily voice purred, "A friend bearing gifts."

"Door's open," I called.

At that the wolf entered the room. Drool trickled from
his mouth. "Surprise, surprise, Granny!" he nearly shouted,
strutting toward me in the bed.

Pretending to be frightened, I quivered and gasped,
"You again!"

The wolf smiled, flashing long, sharp teeth.

He squinted and looked at me more closely.

"Say, Granny," he said. "You look different."

I gulped. "I don't have my lipstick on," I said.

"No," he considered. "It's your feet," he said. "What big feet you have."

I glanced at my feet, which were jammed inside Granny's too-small bunny slippers. "The better to run and greet you," I lied.

"No, it's your voice," the wily wolf said. "What a deep voice you have."

"Nothing a drop of honey tea can't sweeten," I said, coughing slightly.

The wolf licked his lips. "Never mind all this chit-chat," he finally said. "You know why I'm here. I'm going to eat you up."

The wolf stepped closer…and closer…and closer.…Suddenly, I burst out of the bed and grabbed a firm hold of his neck.

Bam! Zing! Zap! The jig was up; the game was over. Like I said, I don't believe in violence but there was just no talking to that wolf.

I knocked on the closet door. "It's safe now, Granny. You can come out."

"But what about that horrible wolf?" she asked.

"Don't worry," I said. "I slam-dunked him into a garbage can. Then he ran away in a hurry. I don't think he'll be back anytime soon."

Relieved, Granny and I sat and sipped honey tea and ate the chocolate chip cookies that the wolf had so kindly delivered. They were, I should mention, delicious. I reminded myself to ask George for the recipe.

I explained to Granny that I was searching for the Hen That Lays Golden Basketballs. Granny's face suddenly brightened. "I have an idea," she said. "You can stop at the emperor's palace. Everyone says he is the wisest man in the land. He might be able to help you find the Hen That Lays Golden Basketballs."

So I said good-bye to Granny, and once again set off through the woods. Little did I realize that I was headed for an unusual—and most embarrassing—visit.

SHAQ AND THE THREE BEARS

WHAT A day.

First I tangled with a giant.

Then I wrestled with a wolf. It was

enough to make me wish I'd stayed home, eaten

those yucky lima beans, and played basketball instead.

Oh well. I had promised the giant that I'd help him find

the Hen That Lays Golden Basketballs. And a promise is a

promise, no matter how ridiculous. So after bidding

George's granny a fond "See ya later, alligator!"

I once again set off into the woods, this time in

search of the emperor's palace.

Well, I hate to say this. But after an

hour, I was lost. That's the problem with

forests. To a kid like me, who didn't

grow up in the country, every step

in the forest looks the same.

Trees ahead of you. Trees

behind you.

I glanced up at the sky. Like a basketball sailing toward the rim, the sun fell in an arc toward the far mountains. I guessed I still had a few more hours of light. One thing was for sure: I did *not* want to be alone in those woods in the dark of night.

So I just put one foot in front of the other and trudged on. Then, off on a distant hill, I saw a small house. Maybe the owners of the house could give me directions to the emperor's palace. And if they had any extra food for a stranger in need, well, I wouldn't turn down a hot stack of pancakes.

The house was painted yellow. A white picket fence surrounded the yard, and a brick walkway led me to the door.

I knocked softly. "Hello?" I called out. "Anybody home?"

No one answered.

"Hello?" I called out in a louder voice. Still no answer. So I sat down on the stoop to think, leaning heavily against the door. *Whoosh! Klunk!* The door swung open. And there I was—my head on the floor and my feet in the air! I jumped up and looked around.

"Hello?" I called out again, wondering what to do. A sudden downpour made my decision easier. I stepped inside to wait for the rain to stop.

It was a real cozy setup. Everything was nice and neat and clean. But there was a strange smell in the air. Like…an animal of some kind. I noticed brown fur on the rug. Must have a dog, I decided. Maybe the owners had taken the pooch out for a walk.

Another smell drifted in from the kitchen. There on the table were three bowls. One small bowl, one medium bowl, and one very large bowl. I leaned over the largest and took a whiff.

Yeech! Porridge!

I hate porridge.

But by now I was very hungry. I decided to whip up a big batch of pancakes. After polishing off a steaming stack of thirteen, I felt better. I got up and went into the living room. There was a small chair, a medium chair, and one very large chair. I tried them all out, but I didn't like any of them. I grabbed the television clicker and sprawled out on the couch. I channel surfed for a while, but then a loud yawn escaped me. *A snooze would be nice*, I thought. So I headed upstairs in search of a comfortable bed.

I found three of them. And yep, you guessed it: One bed was small, one was medium, and one was very large. But I felt weird about sleeping in someone else's bed, so I stretched out on a soft, shaggy rug. In a few minutes, I was asleep.

Now I know—*I just know*—that you're never going to believe the rest of this story. But what can I say? What happened…happened. **Believe it!**

So there I was, sleeping like a baby. Now one thing you have to know about Shaq, and that's when I sleep, I don't mess around. I mean, I *sleep*. Nothing can wake me. Not a hurricane or a tornado. Not even my mother shaking me like a rag doll. When I'm tired, I'm tired. That's all there is to it.

So I guess I didn't exactly hear the bears come into the house.

That's right, I said *bears*.

And nope, I don't mean the Chicago Bears. I'm talking real live bears. The kind with big paws and sharp claws.

Just picture something a whole lot leaner and meaner than Winnie the Pooh and you're on the right track. So like I was saying, I didn't hear the bears come into the house. But I guess they weren't real happy to find pancake batter splattered on the floor, sticky dishes on the table, and butter melting on the counter.

So up they went, into the room where I was snoozing. *Tap, tap.* A large paw softly pushed against my foot.

"Not now, Mom," I mumbled.

Tap, tap, tap. The paw kicked a little harder.

I rolled over with my eyes still closed. "Just a few more minutes, Mom," I complained.

Whap! I felt a good swift kick against the sole of my sneaker. I awoke suddenly and sat up. And there before me stood three bears. A small bear, a medium bear, and a very large bear. *This is not good*, I thought to myself.

41

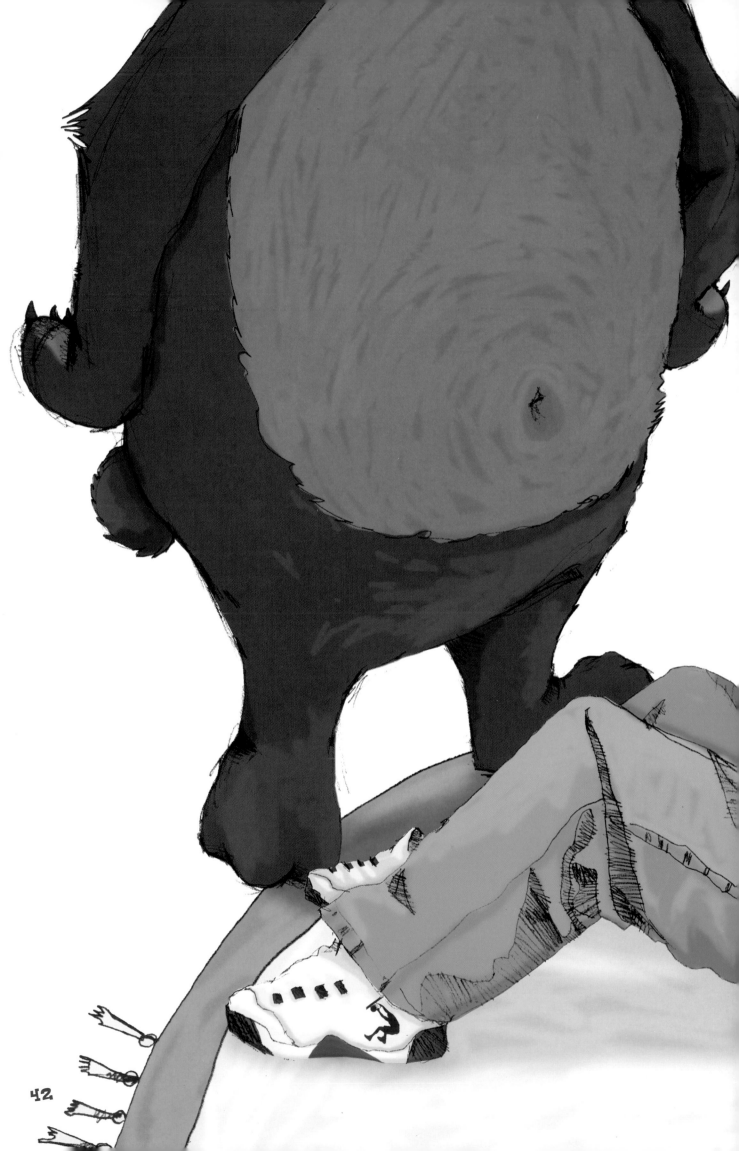

In fact, I thought to myself, *I'm toast.*

The very large bear—he must have been Papa Bear—started pacing back and forth.

"Now see here!" he shouted. Just then, he accidentally banged his paw into the bedpost. "YOWSA!" he screamed. He grabbed his paw and hopped around on one foot. "Mama, where are my glasses? You know I can't see without my glasses!!"

Mama Bear scrambled down the stairs in search of Papa Bear's glasses. Meanwhile, the smallest bear pointed at my head and said in a babyish voice, "Gee, Goldilocks, what happened to your pretty yellow hair?"

"Excuse me?" I said.

The little bear continued, "And Goldilocks, what happened to your pretty blue dress?"

"Say what?" I said. "Who are you calling Goldilocks?"

Papa Bear started in again with his pacing back and forth. "Now, Goldilocks," he said. "You can't fool me with that silly disguise, even without my glasses—I'm smarter than the average bear, you know."

"But I've never seen you in my life," I protested.

But Papa Bear didn't want to listen to my excuses. As for me, well, I didn't know what to think. Except that somehow these bears thought I was Goldilocks.

"The last time you barged in," Papa Bear said, "you gobbled up Baby Bear's porridge...."

"Yeah," chimed in Baby Bear.

"And you broke Baby Bear's chair...."

"That's right," Baby Bear added.

"And then you slept in Baby Bear's bed!"

Finally I jumped up and said, "Now hold on just one minute! I...am...NOT...Goldilocks!"

Papa Bear stopped in his tracks. Baby Bear looked up at me, surprised. And Mama Bear came back into the room, wearing glasses of her own. She handed Papa Bear his glasses. He put them on. He looked at me. He took them off. He cleaned them with a handkerchief. He put them on again.

And very slowly, he backed up a step.

"You're not Goldilocks," he said.

"That's what I've been trying to tell you," I said. "My name is Shaquille O'Neal." I held out my hand. After all, my parents had always taught me to be polite. "Pleased to meet you," I said.

Papa Bear carefully reached out his paw and we shook hands. Or, I mean, we shook paws. Or…oh, you get the idea.

Mama Bear took a seat on the bed. She looked faint. "Better get your mama a glass of water," Papa Bear told the little one. "And you," he said, pointing to me, "have some explaining to do."

So I told him my whole story. I told about the magic lima beans…the giant…the Big Bad Wolf…and how I was in search of the Hen That Lays Golden Basketballs.

Well, I don't think those bears believed a word of it. Instead Mama Bear thought I had a fever or something. She put an ice pack on my head.

All in all, I have to say the bears were pretty nice. When I asked about the emperor's palace, Papa Bear pulled out a telephone book. He flipped through the Yellow Pages and said, "Let's see. This lists two places called the emperor's palace."

I waited patiently, ready to jot down the address.

"You're not talking about the Chinese restaurant, are you?" Papa Bear asked. "They make great egg rolls."

"Nope," I told him.

"Then you must mean the *real* emperor's palace. That sure is some fancy place! Everyone says that the emperor is the wisest man in the land. If anyone knows where your hen ran off to, it's the emperor."

Papa Bear gave me directions to the palace. There was still just enough time to get there before dark if I hurried.

Mama Bear gave me a big hug—I guess you could say it was a bear hug. Baby Bear kept calling me Goldilocks. And Papa Bear, he just clicked the gate closed and invited me back for a honey sandwich anytime I wanted.

I began to run, faster and faster. I was running right into the fading sun. I was on my way to the emperor's palace.

But I was headed right for a heap of trouble.

IT **WAS** as dark as the inside of a cow by
the time I reached the emperor's palace. Still, the full
moon glistened on the golden gates of the palace.
Passing through an iron gate, I entered a wide, grassy
courtyard. What an amazing sight! A thousand candles lit
the scene. Ladies dressed in sparkling gowns strolled
through the town. At their elbows walked handsome men
in fancy clothes.

I noticed a royal guard standing beside a large
golden door. "Excuse me, sir," I said. "I have been
told that the emperor is the wisest man in all
the land."

The guard sniffed and stated simply,
"You have been told correctly, sir."

"Well, I'd like to see him, if you don't
mind," I said.

"I'm afraid that is not possible," the guard told me. "The emperor is busy planning the festivities for the Grand Parade."

I nodded glumly.

"Unless," the guard said, "you know the magic word."

I thought for a minute.

"*Abracadabra?*" I guessed.

The guard shook his head. "Try again," he offered.

Then I snapped my fingers. My mom and dad had taught me the magic word a long time ago. "*Please,*" I said.

The guard instantly stepped aside and threw open the golden door.

I walked down a long hall of mirrors and into a big room.

The walls were filled with
paintings. Each painting was of the
same man. In each one, he was dressed
in colorful clothes, with a golden crown
sparkling on his head.

"Ah, fiddle-dee-dee, a visitor!" I heard a voice call.
"Glorious, just glorious!"

I turned to see the man from the paintings. He didn't look
busy, unless sitting on a throne and staring into a hand mirror is your idea of busy. He wore a long purple robe, striped
trousers, and a frilly shirt. A golden crown sat atop his head.
He was, of course, the emperor.

While I told the emperor my tale, his eyes remained fixed on the mirror. When I finished, the emperor finally looked up and exclaimed, "Fiddle-dee-dee! Golden basketballs! How merry!"

He rang a bell, and his chief minister entered the room. The emperor said to him, "Quickly. Send for the royal hen finders. Tell them to bring me all the hens in the kingdom—at once!"

"But, Your Majesty," the chief minister sputtered. "There are many hens in your great kingdom. This will take weeks."

The emperor waved his hand, "Oh, pish and tosh. I'll give you three days."

The chief minister bowed. He then added, "Your Majesty, two weavers are in the hall. They say that they can weave the most beautiful clothes in all the world."

The emperor clapped his hands together, delighted. He put his arm around my shoulder and said, "Come, Shaquille. In a few days we'll be having the Grand Parade. I insist that you stay as my personal guest. I will give you the honor of walking behind me, holding my long royal robe."

Well, let me tell you, I was pretty confused by that point. I mean, all I did was climb a big old plant—and now I was playing sleepover with an emperor!

The weavers entered the room. For two guys who made beautiful clothes, they weren't dressed all that well.

The first weaver, a tall, thin man, spoke to the emperor. "Your Majesty, we wish to tell you about our amazing, beautiful new cloth."

The second one, who was short and round, added, "It is so beautiful, in fact, that some people cannot even see it."

"Pish and tosh," said the emperor. "What kind of people cannot see it?"

"Rotten people," the short one said.

"And liars," added the tall one.

"Fiddle-dee-dee!" the emperor said. "I must have a suit made out of this amazing new cloth."

The emperor gave the weavers two bags of gold. He sent them to a room where they could make the suit. But before they left, the emperor told them, "And good sirs! Make a suit for my new friend here, Shaquille.

It should be the finest suit—um, the *second* finest suit—in all the kingdom. We will both wear them on the day of the Grand Parade."

With sly smiles, the weavers slithered toward the door.

That night I slept on a mattress filled with the feathers of a thousand geese. I dreamed of George the Giant. I also dreamed of my own home, far away. I woke up homesick. But like my daddy always taught me: A promise is a promise, no matter how ridiculous. I couldn't return home until I found George's prize hen.

At breakfast the emperor rang a bell, and his chief minister entered the room. The emperor sent the chief minister to check up on the weavers. Then he nodded toward me and added, "Take Shaquille along with you!"

In the workroom stood two large wooden looms. The tall, thin weaver raced up to us, waving his arms in great excitement. "Isn't it beautiful?! Isn't it amazing?!"

I looked at the looms. I didn't see any cloth. But after
hesitating for a moment, the chief minister said, "It's gorgeous!"

Now let me stop right here and tell you something. Those
two guys weren't weavers. They were crooks. They were just
pretending to make a suit of beautiful clothes. But the
emperor didn't know that. And I didn't know it, either.
I thought that something was wrong with me. *Am I rotten?*
I asked myself. *Am I a liar?* I didn't think so.

The chief minister told the emperor about the beautiful
cloth. The emperor was thrilled. The next day he sent his
second minister down to the workroom. Once again I tagged
along. It was the same old story. Two big looms with no
cloth in sight. The second minister looked at both looms.

"So…?" asked the short, round weaver. "How do you like our beautiful cloth?"

The second minister rubbed his chin. Finally he said, "Er, oh, yes! I see it now! The colors! The thread! Gorgeous, just gorgeous! " Then he dabbed his forehead with a handkerchief and rushed out of the room. By now, I was very confused. I thought to myself, *Surely I must be rotten.* Because all I saw was a whole lot of nothing!

The night before the Grand Parade, the weavers lit a hundred candles and worked until morning. I watched through the keyhole as they cut the air with scissors and sewed the air with big needles. The rascals smiled while they worked. Now I know why they were smiling. They had tricked the emperor—and they had bags of gold to put smiles on their faces!

At last it was the day of the Grand Parade. The weavers entered the emperor's dressing room. They held out their arms and said, "Here are your new clothes, Your Majesty. And yours, too, Shaquille. Notice that your fine new clothes are as light as a feather."

The weavers sent me to get dressed by myself. Let me tell you, it was pretty weird. I still thought that maybe—*just maybe*—I was wrong. Maybe the clothes were beautiful, but I just couldn't see them. So I took off all my clothes except for my boxers and an undershirt and pretended to get dressed. Meanwhile, I heard the weavers talking to the emperor.

"Here are your fine trousers and your royal cape," the round one said.

"Your new suit is so light," the skinny one said, "it will hardly feel like you are wearing anything at all." The short, round one snickered. "Hate to dress you and run," he said. "But we must be off."

I listened as the weavers tore out of the emperor's dressing room. Their feet pounded down the long hallway and out the castle door.

The Grand Parade started. A crowd of people lined the street. You see, by that time, word had gotten around the kingdom. Everybody wanted to see the emperor's—and Shaq's—new clothes. At last, out stepped the emperor with his head held high. And there I was behind him, holding up a royal cape...that wasn't really there.

"Look!" everyone cried. They pointed at us and called out, "What beautiful new clothes!"

Believe it! This is how I figure it: Nobody could really see the clothes. The emperor and I were just a couple of dudes walking around in our underwear! But I guess no one wanted the emperor to think they were rotten.

So everyone pretended to see the clothes…except for one small girl. She pointed at us and said to her mother, "Why are those guys in their underwear?"

"The child said the emperor is in his underwear," a voice in the crowd said.

One person said it, then another, then another.

Oh, boy.

See, that minute, I knew. We'd been tricked, deceived, and bamboozled. I looked at the emperor and he looked at me. We were both embarrassed. But the emperor said, "Oh, phooey. It's all pish and tosh. The Grand Parade must go on."

So slowly, proudly—though, admittedly, with a bit of a chill—we marched through the crowd.

After the Grand Parade (and after we put on some real clothes), the emperor pulled me aside. "Shaquille," he said, "for three days, my royal hen finders have searched the land. Let us see what they have found."

Well, you wouldn't believe the racket—here a cluck, there a cluck, everywhere a cluck, cluck! I'd never seen so many hens in all my life. But there were no hens that laid golden basketballs. The emperor, who, I now realized, was more kind than wise, saw that I was disappointed.

"Shaquille," he said, "there is one last place you must look. But it is dangerous."

The emperor called for his royal mapmaker. In an instant, we were staring down at a large map. The emperor pointed to a black patch called the Forbidden Zone.

"Here, under this bridge," the emperor said, "lives the meanest troll that has ever walked the land. My royal hen finders dared not cross over his bridge. That might be where you'll find your hen." The emperor paused, "That is, if it is not too late."

"Too late?" I asked.

"Yes," said the emperor. "Unlike me, the troll likes to eat his guests!"

As I prepared to leave, the emperor pinned a medal on my chest. "This medal is for bravery," he said, "for only the bravest in the land would dare face the troll."

I turned my back on the emperor and headed for the Forbidden Zone, prepared to meet the meanest troll in all the land.

I only hoped that I wouldn't end up as dessert.

SHAQ AND THE THREE BILLY GOATS GRUFF

YOU'VE HEARD the story of "The Three Billy Goats Gruff"? Well, this one is a little different. Because in this story, there is a *fourth* billy goat. That's right—you guessed it. Me!

Believe it!

I followed the emperor's map until I came to the Forbidden Zone. I knew I was there because there was a huge sign with blinking lights that read FORBIDDEN ZONE.

There were other signs, too, hanging on trees and fence posts.

KEEP OUT!

DANGER

FORBIDDEN ZONE

WE'RE NOT KIDD...

BEWARE OF TROLL

This is it, I thought to myself. The moment of truth.
I mean, I could have turned around and skedaddled on home.
After all, who was George the Giant to me, anyway? Just a
big guy with a bad attitude. But for
some reason, I liked George. And
like I always said, a promise is a
promise, no matter how
ridiculous.

I knew I was near the troll's bridge when I started to find bones scattered along the path. Let me tell you, it wasn't a pretty sight.

Then I came upon three billy goats, huddled together on a field of stones and dirt. They were so old and thin, their bones rattled when they walked.

I stopped before them. "Excuse me," I asked, "is this the way to the troll's bridge?"

The oldest billy goat stepped forward. "Yes, it is," he said. "But if you value your life, you will turn around now."

I gazed down the road. There I saw a bridge that led across to a fine meadow of grass and flowers. I looked again at the three skinny billy goats.

Without a word, I pulled out the bag the emperor had given me for my journey. It was filled with tasty sandwiches, fine pastries, and sticky taffy. I took a sandwich for myself and placed the rest on the ground. "Anyone hungry?" I asked. "I hate to eat alone."

Snip, snap, snout! I'd never seen food disappear so quickly. The hungry brothers Gruff ate everything except the taffy.

"Gets stuck in my choppers," the oldest explained.

"Rots your teeth," added the youngest.

After we ate, the brothers told me their sad tale. For many years the Three Billy Goats Gruff crossed the bridge each day to feed.

"What about the mean old troll?" I asked.

The oldest brother Gruff explained, "Once I was large and strong. My two horns were like iron fists. My four hard hooves could trample a mountain." He sighed then, as goats often do, and said, "But I have grown weak. I can no longer protect my brothers. The troll will not let us pass. So here we sit, slowly starving to death."

Man, that story made me mad. I mean, how could anybody be so nasty as that rotten troll? I decided that I'd find a way to help those three brothers Gruff, or my name wasn't Shaquille O'Neal.

Together, we formed a plan. I could only hope it would work—because I sure didn't want *my* bones on the side of the road.

I hid behind a rock and watched as the youngest Billy Goat Gruff crossed the bridge.

"Clip, Clop, Clip, Clop!" went the bridge.

"WHO'S MAKING ALL THAT RACKET?" roared the angry troll.

"Oh dear, oh my, it is only I," said the youngest brother Gruff. "I'm going to the meadow."

"NO HOW, NO WAY!" screamed the troll from beneath the bridge. "I'M COMING UP TO CHEW ON YOUR BONES!"

"Oh goodness, no," said the youngest brother Gruff. "Wait until my older brother comes across. He'd make a much better meal."

"GO AHEAD!" roared the troll. "AND BE QUIET WITH ALL THE CLIP-CLOPPING. YOU GOATS GIVE ME SUCH A HEADACHE!"

In a few minutes the second brother began to cross the bridge.

"*Clip, Clop, Clip, Clop!*" groaned the bridge.

"WHO'S MAKING ALL THAT RACKET?" roared the angry troll.

"Oh dear, oh my, it is only I," said the second brother Gruff. "I'm going to the meadow."

"NO HOW, NO WAY, NOT TODAY!" screamed the troll.

"I'M COMING UP TO CHEW ON YOUR BONES!"

"Wait until the third Billy Goat Gruff comes across," pleaded the second brother. "He'd make a much better meal."

"GO AHEAD!" roared the troll. "AND HURRY UP! ALL THAT CLIP-CLOPPING GIVES ME A HEADACHE!"

At last, the oldest Billy Goat Gruff clomped across the bridge.

"Clip, Clop, Clip, Clop!" sounded the bridge.

"AH, FINALLY!" roared the angry troll. "HERE COMES MY NEXT MEAL!"

"Oh heavens, no," said the oldest brother Gruff. "I'm just fur and bones. Wait for the fourth Billy Goat Gruff. He's the fattest one of all."

"*FOUR* BILLY GOATS GRUFF?" hollered the troll. "I THOUGHT THERE WERE ONLY THREE OF YOU GUYS!"

"Oh yes, four indeed," answered the oldest brother Gruff. "The fattest brother Gruff has been away at the emperor's palace, eating fine meals each day. And, I might add, *he looks delicious!"*

"GO AHEAD, THEN!" roared the troll. "I'LL EAT THE FATTEST ONE OF ALL!"

I watched as the three brothers Gruff safely scampered up the hillside. Next it was my turn.

Earlier I had clipped some fur from each of the goats. Now I quickly stuck the fur to my clothes, using the sticky taffy from the emperor. It worked like a charm. That taffy was stickier than superglue! I stuck a long white beard to my chin. Then I shoved the bag of taffy into my back pocket. And—*clip-clop*—headed over the bridge.

Suddenly the troll leaped onto the bridge and stood before me, slime dribbling from his long, sharp teeth. "NOW I'M GOING TO CHEW ON YOUR BONES!" the troll roared.

"I'm afraid that's so," I said. "But tell me first, have you stolen any hens lately?"

"HOW WOULD I KNOW?" roared the troll. "HENS, GOATS, LITTLE MEN — IT'S ALL THE SAME TO ME!" He moved closer.

"But this hen," I said, "is different. She lays golden basketballs."

The troll smiled fiendishly. "YES, I HAVE HER IN A CAGE BELOW. THE EGGS ARE GOLD, IT'S TRUE." He burped and added, "YUMMY IN MY TUMMY!"

At this, I heard a few fearful clucks coming from beneath the bridge. I shivered, hoping that my trick would work. "Okay," I said. "You can chow down on me if you want.

But since everyone says you are a fair and honest troll, at least let me have a final meal." I pulled out the taffy.

"FAIR AND HONEST!" screamed the troll. "HOW DARE YOU CALL ME SUCH A TERRIBLE THING!" His glowing green eyes fixed upon the bag of taffy. "WHAT IS THAT?" he asked.

"It's the most delicious treat I've ever tasted," I answered. "And I'm not sharing."

"NOT SHARING?" ranted the troll. In an instant, he snatched the whole bag of sticky taffy from my hand and shoved it into his mouth.

I watched and waited. The expression on the troll's hideous face changed from triumph...to concern...to outright fear. Because the troll had glued his great mouth shut! (I *told* you it was really sticky taffy.)

"WHHHATTSSHH ISSTHH THISSTH SSTHHUUUUFF?" he mumbled, unable to get the words out.

"Taffy," I answered. "It rots your teeth. You will never chew on another bone for as long as you live."

At this news the troll tried to pry open his mouth. Grunting and groaning, he rolled on the bridge in a wild rage.

After a while, he stopped. He knew he'd been tricked. And I didn't feel one bit sorry for him.

"Scat!" I screamed, stomping on the bridge. The troll leaped up and ran across the bridge, through the valley, and over the hillside. No one, as far as I know, has seen him since.

I climbed down and grabbed the Hen That Lays Golden Basketballs. She clucked nervously.

"Don't worry," I whispered. "I'm here to save you."

I waved good-bye to the brothers Gruff, who were eating happily in the meadow. Then I looked down at the hen. "Come on," I said. "Let's go see George. It's time for both of us to go home."

I MADE it back to the giant's castle in no time flat. Once again I rapped on the huge wooden door.

To say that George was happy to see his beloved hen is like saying it gets a little chilly in Antarctica. George was more than happy. He was nearly crazy with happiness! He scooped me up, twirled me around, and nearly hugged me to death.

After George calmed down, he said, "Shaq, I was wrong about you. Not all Little People are big trouble."

I told George that it was no big deal. Thing is, I don't really like it when people make a big fuss. Sure, I did the right thing—but that's what people are supposed to do. And besides, it's not like I didn't have fun. I got to outwit the Big Bad Wolf…hang out with the three bears…march in a parade with a real live emperor…and trick a nasty troll. What an adventure!

But now I was eager to get home. My parents were probably worried—and I sure did miss them.

Before I left, George gave me a golden basketball. I thanked him and climbed down that crazy lima bean stalk. Down I went. Through the clouds, past the tops of trees, until I finally reached the ground. Home sweet home.

Now here's the funny thing. When I got home, I was pretty confused. The kitchen wall clock read 9:15. It was still morning. Was it all a dream? I raced to the window. The lima bean stalk was…*gone*.

"Where's the giant beanstalk?" I asked.

My dad, Sarge, looked at me like I was crazy. My mom only laughed and said, "Oh, Shaquille, that imagination of yours is really running wild this morning."

Okay, I'll tell you, it was all pretty weird. And I guess I would have believed it was all just a dream. Except for one thing. When I left the house later that morning, I walked out into the garden. You know what I found, right?

Yep, a golden basketball.

I still have it to this very day.

Believe it!

And that, as they say, is all he wrote.

The final buzzer.

THE END

Um, er, what's that you say?

You don't believe my stories?

You think they are tall tales?
Well, okay, sure. Maybe I did
s-t-r-e-t-c-h the truth a bit.
Maybe they are TALL tales.
But hey, what do you
expect from a guy who is over
seven feet tall?
Short tales?!
I don't think so!

THE END

(Believe it!)